MARVEL

THE AVENGERS

™

All for One!

Part 1

adapted by Michael Teitelbaum

based on the Marvel comic book series *The Mighty Avengers*

interior illustrated by Pat Olliffe and Hi-Fi Design

Reader's Digest
Children's Books®

MARVEL
marvelkids.com

New York, New York • Montréal, Québec • Bath, United Kingdom

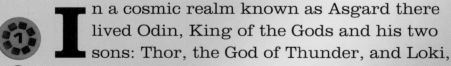

1 In a cosmic realm known as Asgard there lived Odin, King of the Gods and his two sons: Thor, the God of Thunder, and Loki, the God of Mischief. Being the elder of the two brothers, Thor was next in line to sit on the throne of Asgard.

2 This made Loki furious and very jealous. Loki hoped that he could become King of the Gods of Asgard. But every attempt to get rid of Thor

ended in disaster for Loki. Finally, Thor asked

3 Odin's permission to banish Loki. Odin agreed.

And so it was that Loki was banished to the
Isle of Silence. Loki was full of tricks, though.

4 He could send visions across great distances and
plant them in the minds of others, making them
see things that did not exist.

He planned to do this to Thor. But first Loki
had to find his brother.

Loki used his great mental powers to search all the realms of the universe. In time, he found Thor on the planet Earth.

⑤ "Thor is such a fool," Loki grumbled to himself. "He is a god. He should be ruling these weak Earth creatures, not serving as their champion.

And there are others on Earth who call themselves heroes."

Loki's mind reached out to Thor, but he found himself blocked. "Bah! I should have known that I could not attack Thor directly," Loki muttered. "He is under the protection of our father Odin."

"I must bring Thor to the Isle of Silence,"
Loki snarled. "Here I can defeat him. If I can
find a simple-minded, yet powerful creature
that I can control, I can draw Thor out and stop
his misguided attempts to protect humans."

Searching Earth, Loki found the Hulk near
some railroad tracks. He planted a vision of
⑦ broken, twisted train tracks in the Hulk's mind.

"Tracks busted!" cried the Hulk. "Train will crash. People will be hurt. Hulk can help them. Hulk will stop train!"

With that, the Hulk bounded high into the air. He landed on the tracks and tried to stop the train.

On board the train, the startled conductor spotted the Hulk on the tracks ahead and slammed on the brakes. The train screeched and slowed, but would not be able to stop before hitting the muscular monster in its path.

Bracing himself for the impact, the Hulk met the oncoming train. The Hulk's incredible strength allowed him to stop the train before it hit the broken tracks. Satisfied that he had saved the people on the train, the Hulk bounded away.

But there was actually nothing wrong with the train tracks! To everyone else, it appeared that the Hulk had attacked the train for no reason.

Word of the Hulk's attack on the train spread quickly.

Among those who saw the TV news was Dr. Donald Blake, who in reality was the mortal form of Loki's brother—the Thunder God, Thor. Tapping his cane on the ground, Donald Blake changed into Thor. His cane transformed into Thor's mighty hammer, Mjolnir.

Thor spun Mjolnir and allowed it to lift him into the sky. He set off to find the Hulk.

At the same time, billionaire industrialist Tony Stark was in his office when news came of the attack.

Hmm, he thought. *There's more to this than meets the eye.*

Tony Stark decided to investigate—as Iron Man. Slipping into his hi-tech metal armor, Iron Man sped to the spot where the crumpled remains of the train sat smoldering.

But Iron Man was surprised to find that he was not the only super-powered being at the scene.

③   Ant-Man and the Wasp were already investigating the train crash by the time Iron Man arrived.

"Where is the Hulk?" Iron Man asked.

④   "He's gone," replied the Wasp.

"He fled," Ant-Man explained.

At that moment, Thor came drifting down from above. "I am Thor, God of Thunder, and I am here to lend my assistance to the mortals of Earth," he announced.

"Well, the first thing we need is to figure out where the Hulk went," Iron Man explained.

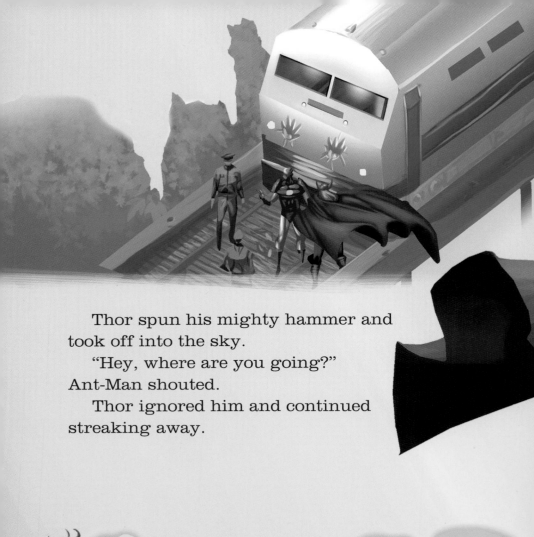

Thor spun his mighty hammer and took off into the sky.

"Hey, where are you going?" Ant-Man shouted.

Thor ignored him and continued streaking away.

Thor had spotted the Hulk nearby. What he did not know was that the Hulk was really many miles away. Loki had placed the image of the Hulk into Thor's mind.

"Stop, Hulk!" Thor shouted. "I must speak with you!"

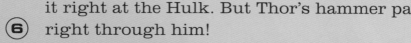

(5)   Thor finally tracked down the Hulk. The Thunder God spun his mighty hammer then flung it right at the Hulk. But Thor's hammer passed (6) right through him!

"It is merely an illusion!" Thor cried as Mjolnir returned to his hand.

Then the image of the Hulk faded, replaced for a brief moment by the smirking face of Loki.

"This entire plot is the work of my brother!" Thor said, standing alone in the lot. "I must return to Asgard at once!"

Iron Man, Ant-Man, and the Wasp had
followed Thor. They were stunned to see Thor
flinging his hammer at nothing.

They watched Thor take off and fly away.
Within seconds he had disappeared into the sky.

"It's more important to find the Hulk than to
follow Thor," Iron Man said.

"But how will we find him?" the Wasp asked.

"I have an idea," Ant-Man replied. "I can mentally contact ants all over the world. I'll have the ants search for the Hulk wherever he is."

"Ants?" Iron Man asked in disbelief.

"That's right," Ant-Man replied.

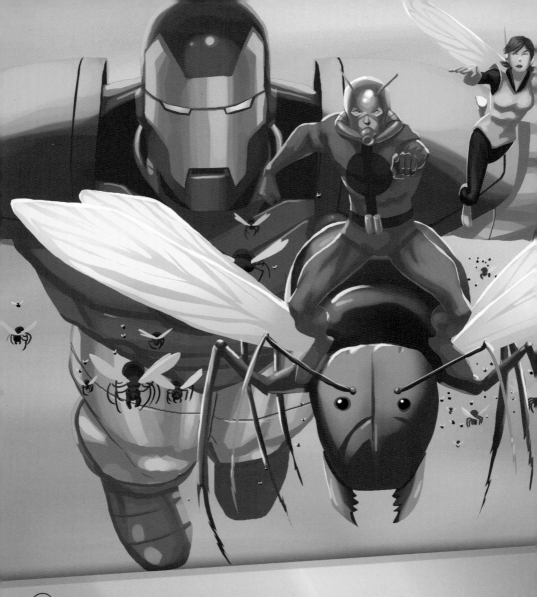

8 "I'm receiving a signal from some ants!" Ant-Man said excitedly.

Riding aboard a flying ant, Ant-Man took off into the sky. The Wasp and Iron Man followed closely behind.

"Where are we going?" Iron Man asked.

"Just follow me," Ant-Man insisted. "I'll let you know when we're there."

To be continued...